DISNEP'S

Family Storybook Library

A Family Is Your Most Precious Possession

Stories About Family

BOOK ONE

For information address Disney Press,
114 Fifth Avenue, New York, New York 10011-5690.

First Edition
1 3 5 7 9 10 8 6 4 2

ISBN: 0-7868-5866-4

"Cruella's Wicked Puppy Plan" is based on
the original book *The One Hundred and One Dalmatians* by
Dodie Smith, published by Viking Press.

A Family Is Your Most Precious Possession

Stories About Family

Introduction

Everyone feels the need to belong, whether it's to
a circle of friends, a social group, a church, or a club.
Children, especially, want to know that they fit in.
They need to feel secure about their place in the world
around them. A family is often the first group in
which children feel that sense of belonging. A family,
whether it is made up of parents and siblings or aunts,
uncles, and cousins, can provide both a refuge and
a springboard to new experiences.

While Pinocchio's family is unorthodox, Pinocchio
loves Geppetto as a son loves a father. And Perdita
and Pongo may not be human, but they love and
protect their pups as fiercely as any parent could.
Whatever the shape and size of your family, it's your
most precious possession!

A Whale of a Tale

from *Pinocchio*

When you love someone,
their life can mean more to you than your own.

To become a real boy, all the wooden puppet, Pinocchio, had to do was be brave, truthful, and unselfish. But he was having trouble living up to any of those ideals. He had already lied to the Blue Fairy. And then he had been weak and

selfish by going to Pleasure Island, where he had smoked cigars, played pool, and almost been turned into a donkey.

Ashamed, Pinocchio swam back to the mainland with Jiminy Cricket. Outside Geppetto's workshop, Pinocchio cried, "Father! Father, I'm home!"

No one answered. Geppetto was gone. And, from the look of the dust and cobwebs, he had been gone awhile.

As Pinocchio and Jiminy sat outside, a dove dropped a piece of paper at their feet. The note said that Geppetto had gone looking for Pinocchio and been swallowed by a whale named Monstro. Apparently Geppetto was still alive inside the whale, which was resting at the bottom of the sea.

"I'm going to find my father," Pinocchio

declared. "I'm going to the bottom of the sea."

On a high cliff, Pinocchio tied a heavy rock to his tail. Jiminy grabbed hold of the rope and plunged into the water with Pinocchio.

At the bottom of the sea, Jiminy grabbed a smaller rock to use as a weight. Pinocchio wandered into a school of fish, and before he knew it, he was swept into the whale's belly.

Pinocchio saw his father sitting forlornly in his fishing boat. "Father!" cried Pinocchio. "I've come to save you."

"No, Pinocchio. There's no way out. Monstro only opens his mouth when he's eating. Then everything comes in—nothing goes out."

Pinocchio thought hard. "Father! We'll build a big fire, and the smoke will make Monstro sneeze!"

They started a blaze with some of the wood from Geppetto's boat.

As the flames grew, Pinocchio and

Geppetto hastily built a raft with the
remaining wood.

The whale shook, then sneezed. The
tremendous force sent the little raft hurtling
out of Monstro's mouth.

The furious whale swam beneath the raft

and thrust it into the air. Geppetto and
Pinocchio tumbled into the sea. "Hurry,
Father!" cried Pinocchio.

"I can't make it, son. Save yourself."

"No, Father, I won't leave you!" Pinocchio
grabbed Geppetto's shirt and dragged him

to shore. There was no way he was going to lose sight of his father now.

Later, after both Pinocchio and Geppetto were safely at home, the Blue Fairy rewarded Pinocchio by making him into a real boy. He had proven himself brave, truthful, and unselfish.

Cruella's Wicked Puppy Plan

from *101 Dalmatians*

Nothing is stronger than a parent's love.

t was a cold, dark night. The snow swirled and the wind blew, but Pongo and Perdita raced across the countryside with only one thought on their minds: They had to save their puppies!

Cruella De Vil had stolen their puppies,

and many more besides. She had hidden
them in an old house far from London. She
planned to make Dalmatian coats out of
them!

With a ferocious growl, Pongo leaped
into the house where the puppies were kept.
Perdita showed the ninety-nine puppies
how to escape, while Pongo bravely snapped

and jumped
at Cruella's
dim-witted
henchmen.
Once the
puppies were
safely outside,
Pongo and
Perdita led them
away from the
De Vil house.

The snow was
deep, making it
hard for the

group to go very fast. Pongo and Perdita knew that Cruella would be after them.

To make sure they didn't leave pawprints in the snow, Pongo and Perdita had the puppies follow them on a frozen stream. Soon the headlights from Cruella's car shone in the darkness. The Dalmatian family had to hide under a bridge.

"That was a close one, Perdy," Pongo said.

"I'm c-c-c-cold," Lucky said, shivering.

"And I'm hungry," said Rolly.

Pongo and Perdita brought the puppies to a barn, where they all rested for the night. The cows had never seen so many dogs in one place. They happily shared their milk with the puppies.

In the morning, the dogs were on their way again. Cruella was still looking for them,

so they hid in an old blacksmith's shop. Soon
the playful puppies were romping around in
the ashes.

"That gives me an idea!" Pongo cried.
"Come on, everybody, roll in the soot. I want

all of you good and dirty!"

Shortly after, one hundred and one black dogs nervously marched across the street, right under Cruella's nose. The plan had worked! The dogs were able to board a truck bound for London, and were soon on their way home.

Roger and Anita were very surprised when they heard Pongo barking at the door.

"Pongo, old boy! Is it really you?" Roger cried when they ran in. The house was quickly filled with happy, dirty, playful puppies.

"But, Roger, what will we do with them all?" Anita asked.

"We'll keep them!" Roger cried. "Families stick together!"